Naughty STORIES for Good boys and girls

CHRISTOPHER MILNE

The Girl with Death Breath
and Other Naughty Stories for Good Boys and Girls
published in 2011 by
Hardie Grant Egmont
85 High Street
Prahran, Victoria 3181, Australia
www.hardiegrantegmont.com.au

A CiP record for this title is available from the National Library of Australia

Text copyright © 2011 Christopher Milne
Illustration and design copyright © 2011 Hardie Grant Egmont

Illustration and design by Simon Swingler
Typesetting by Ektavo
Printed in Australia

1 3 5 7 9 10 8 6 4 2

Other books by Christopher Milne
The Day Our Teacher Went Mad and Other Naughty Stories
The Bravest Kid I've Ever Known and Other Naughty Stories
The Girl Who Blew Up Her Brother and Other Naughty Stories
An Upside-Down Boy and Other Naughty Stories
That Dirty Dog and Other Naughty Stories
The Crazy Dentist and Other Naughty Stories
The Toilet Rat of Terror and Other Naughty Stories

Also available from www.christophermilne.com.au
The Western Sydney Kid
Little Johnnie and the Naughty Boat People

the girl with death breath

-AND- OTHER

Naughty STORIES for Good boys and girls

CHRISTOPHER·MILNE

Illustrations by
Simon Swingler

hardie grant EGMONT

TO PETE AND ROB

Peter and Robert are my two sons and they
provided the inspiration for most of my stories.
They have always been a bit naughty in
real life, but also brave, clever, decent
and funny – and much-loved.

Pete and Rob went to Nayook Primary School
and many of these stories are loosely
based on those wonderful years.

Christopher Milne

Contents

the girl with death breath

Doris Katz had the worst breath in the history of the universe. Worse than my dog's. Worse than my father's in the morning.

Butt-breath, we called her.

How did it get so bad? I'll tell you.

It all began with a party – the first that any

of us had been to with both boys and girls.

My best friend, Cassandra Watts, had decided it was time we had a 'real' party and, unfortunately, that meant asking stupid boys. And boys really are stupid.

At the start of the party, we girls were all dressed up, sitting in the lounge room, waiting to maybe talk or dance or something, and what were the idiot boys doing?

Having burping competitions around the barbeque. And every now and then, doing a pop-off.

Eventually, Cassandra realised the party was going nowhere, so she decided to organise some games. Guess what she suggested?

Spin the bottle.

For those of you who haven't played it, that's where a boy spins the bottle and he has to kiss the girl it points to. In front of everyone.

Cassandra had seen her older sister play it and thought it was very grown-up.

We all groaned. I looked at that burping, smelly bunch of losers and thought, *There's certainly no one there I want to kiss.*

But Cassandra insisted.

And so the game began. Roger Smith was the first. The bottle spun, then slowed, and all the girls squealed as the bottle stopped – on Doris Katz!

'Oh, no!' screamed Doris.

But, secretly, we all knew Doris would have been rapt. She'd always liked Roger.

'Do I have to?' pleaded Doris.

'Yes!' we all shrieked.

So, Roger walked over to Doris and put his arm around her waist – just like on TV! He opened his mouth, poked out his tongue, and, as we all leant forward to watch, he moved to kiss her.

But then Roger stopped. 'Oh, yuck!' he shouted. 'Your breath stinks. What have you been eating?'

'I don't know,' said poor Doris. 'Nothing.'

'I'd rather kiss my dog,' said Roger.

Well, I've seen people embarrassed before, but never as badly as poor Doris. She went red, put her hands to her face, and ran crying from the room.

When Doris told her parents what had happened, minus the bottle-spinning, her mum took her to the doctor. But the doctor said there was nothing wrong with Doris. Perhaps she could clean her teeth a little more regularly, but the doctor thought it was simply a case of boys being stupid.

So Doris went off to school thinking the whole thing would soon be forgotten.

5

But it wasn't.

Pretty soon, every single kid at school was calling her **Dunny-Breath** or **Death-Breath**, and pretending to choke every time she came near. Doris's life became a misery. Then misery turned to anger.

OK, thought Doris one day. *I've had enough. If it's bad breath they want, it's* **bad breath** *they'll get!*

So, for the next month, Doris ate smelly cheese, onions and garlic every day – and didn't clean her teeth once. She also practised sleeping with her mouth open and deliberately wore as little clothing as possible, so that

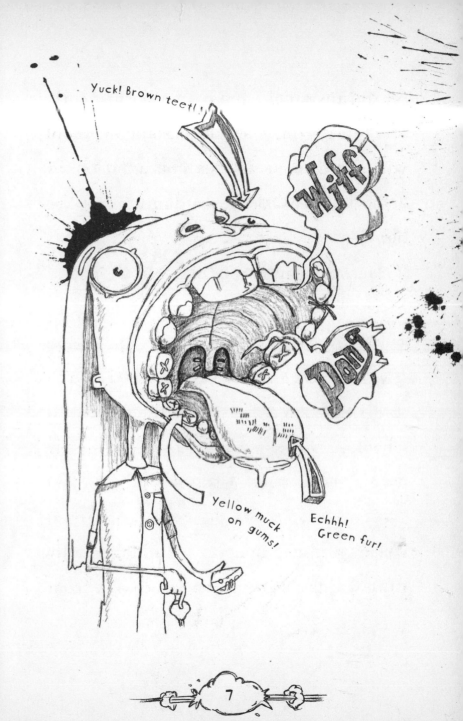

she'd catch a cold and have a permanently sore throat. Finally, she drank some week-old milk, and then opened her mouth and looked in the mirror. What she saw almost made her throw up.

Her throat was red, her **teeth were brown**, there was yellow in between them, and worst of all, her tongue had grown some **green fur**.

She grinned at herself, and then went to school.

Doris's plan had been to say a big, breathy **hello** right into everyone's face. But from

the moment she arrived at school, she could tell something was wrong.

A big group of kids were gathered in a circle. In the middle, Doris could see Roger – whom she still secretly liked – and Kevin 'Killer' Krump. They were shouting at each other and she could just tell a fight was going to start.

Poor Roger, thought Doris. *He won't have a chance against Killer. He's huge. And nasty.*

So, Doris pushed her way to the front, with her mouth closed, and stood right next to Killer. Just as Killer pushed Roger in the chest and said, 'Come on!', and Roger pushed him back, Doris quietly took in a

giant lungful of air.

Then, ever so softly, she blew it right into Killer's face.

Killer stopped, shook his head and started to sweat. He went limp, turned red, then green, and then finally, with his eyes rolling to the back of his head, **passed out cold**.

'Yes,' screamed the other kids.

'He's scared!'

'Too good for him, Roger!'

Doris and Roger are good friends these days. And do you know what? They've even had a kiss.

Doris cleans her teeth regularly, too.
Although sometimes she finds it a bit hard.
Eleven times a day is a lot.

maybe millionaires

When Penny and Michelle Dyer's dad started crying at the dinner table because he'd lost his job, they decided to do something about it.

The Dyers never seemed to have any money as it was. Their house looked as if

it was falling down around their ears, and their car had had it. Plus the girls could never afford things like movies or lollies and they always had to wear their neighbour's hand-me-downs. Not that they complained about it. Why make things worse?

Mr Dyer had often said, 'Who knows what we'd do if I lost this job?' Secretly, Penny and Michelle knew exactly what they'd do. Earn some money themselves, to help out. But they'd never tell their dad. It would probably hurt his feelings.

So, that night, Penny and Michelle lay in their bunks, and talked and talked and talked. Penny had heard on the radio that a man

had become a millionaire by finding bits of old junk, fixing them up and selling them. Simple as that.

'Excellent,' said Michelle. 'I've always wanted to be a millionaire.'

Every few months in the area where they lived, there was a special day when people threw out all their old stuff that didn't normally go in a rubbish bin. Things like old toys, old prams, tyres, bits of tin, boxes and stuff – you name it.

If you looked hard enough, you could usually find just about anything. People would leave all the old stuff out on a Sunday, and by Monday afternoon it would all be gone,

collected by people from the council in big trucks.

Luckily, a throw-out day was coming up the very next afternoon. By the time the sun was starting to rise, Michelle could hardly contain herself. 'Imagine,' she said, getting really excited, 'by this time tomorrow we'll be millionaires.'

'I don't think it's quite that easy,' said Penny with a yawn, 'but we'll certainly give it a try. What we need to do is catch a bus to one of the really rich areas because their junk will be the best.'

'Catch a bus? By ourselves!' said Michelle. 'Mum would kill us.'

'Not if she doesn't know,' said Penny.

So later that morning, Penny and Michelle ended up walking down a leafy street past some of the biggest houses you could ever imagine. And Penny was right. Out on the nature strips stood piles of the most beautiful rubbish the girls had ever seen. Toys, furniture, electrical stuff. Everything. The first thing to really catch Penny's eye was an old ten-pin bowling ball.

'Look at this!' yelled Penny. 'Fill in these cracks with chewy or something and it's as good as new. And look! False teeth! They're worth heaps, aren't they?'

The girls found stacks of stuff. They used

an old wheelbarrow to carry everything —
toys, plates, even a blanket with fewer holes
than the ones they had at home.

'No way we're selling this,' said Penny.
'Give it to Mum. Remember how cold she
got last winter?'

They also found a fan that probably didn't
work, but who knew, maybe if they hit it
with a hammer a couple of times it'd come
good. And a toilet brush that looked pretty
good, although Michelle thought they should
come back for it later in case they found a
better one.

And then they saw it. Neither of them
could believe their eyes. A huge television

set! Michelle and Penny's family hadn't had a TV since the old one blew and, in Michelle's eyes, here was half a million bucks just waiting to be carried away.

'Do you think it still works?' Penny whispered in awe.

'Yes, it does,' said a lady's voice from behind. The girls got such a fright they almost jumped out of their skins.

'Sorry,' said Penny, 'we just –'

'No need to be sorry,' said the lady. 'It looks like you've got quite the haul there!'

When Penny explained how they were going to be millionaires to help out their dad, the lady almost cried.

'Well,' she said, 'there's nothing that pleases me more than people showing some courage. People trying their best. How about I ask my husband to put the trailer on the car and I give you a lift with all of this stuff?'

'I don't want to sound rude or anything,' said Penny, 'but Mum and Dad always say not to get into cars with people we don't know.'

'And very good advice it is, too,' said the lady. 'Silly of me not to think. What if you tell me where your place is, and I'll just take the stuff for you? Oh, and if you'd like to give me your telephone number, I think I might have a few more things I could give you to sell.'

'Radical,' said Penny. 'We haven't got a

phone at the moment but the shop at the end of the street will usually take messages for us.'

'That sounds fine,' said the lady. 'My name's Carmel, by the way.'

'Nice to meet you,' the girls said.

The lady dropped all the stuff at a park near the girls' house, and by that afternoon the girls had their shop all set up. Guess how many things they sold?

None. **Not one.** They had never been so disappointed in all their lives.

'Isn't anyone using false teeth anymore?' asked Penny. 'I can't believe it. Still, at least we get to keep the TV for ourselves.'

'What do we do now?' wondered Michelle.

'Leave the whole lot here, I suppose,' said Penny. 'Let the council pick it up in the morning.'

As the girls trudged into their house, they were most surprised to hear the sound of laughter.

'You'll never guess,' squealed their mum. 'Your dad's got a job. A really good one. With better pay and everything.'

'Mum, that's so fantastic,' said Penny. 'Who with?'

'With a lady called Carmel, doing repairs and odd jobs and gardening,' said her mum. 'It's unbelievable. Apparently she'd heard

what a good worker your father is and how he's really keen on gardening, and she just rang up the shop and offered him a job.'

'How terrific,' said the girls, looking at each other. Although, of course, they would never tell that they knew who the lady was.

Whether their dad knew their secret, the girls never found out. But he did spend a chunk of his first paycheck on two beautiful new dresses.

the toughest kid in school

Bulldog Brown was tough. Very tough. If he told you to nick off, you wouldn't hang around to ask why. If he punched you — which was often — you'd say, 'Good hit, Bulldog.'

I didn't like him. Not at all. Not because he was tough — someone is always going to be

the toughest in every school. It was because he picked on the little kids. And I hated that.

It was when Bulldog belted up my brother Robbie that did it. No-one hits my little brother! Except me, of course, but that's different. I have to put up with him all the time.

Yes, Bulldog was a bully. It was time to teach him a lesson. I asked my mate, Nicholas Rowney, 'How can we get Bulldog? How can we fix him up so he'll never hurt anyone again?'

Nick wasn't too sure but he agreed that something definitely had to be done.

'The first step,' said Nick, 'would be to

get the old Underground Cubby Club back together again. We used to be able to fix anything!'

What an excellent idea, I thought. I'm surprised I didn't think of it myself.

The Underground Cubby Club was a group of eight kids. We built the most excellent underground cubby you could ever imagine. There were secret entrances, secret chambers, secret everything. In fact, I'm really not allowed to tell you too much about it. Gee, we had some fun.

But it all ended when the land on top of the cubby was bulldozed for houses. Once the cubby was gone, somehow the club went

too. I sometimes get drips in my eyes when I think about it.

Do you know the thing I remember most? The smell of the dirt. It was almost sweet. Somehow it used to make me excited. Sort of nervous. I suppose it's because we had so many excellent times.

The other thing I remember best had to do with smell. Yes, you guessed it. Somehow we never got tired of laughing when someone let one go underground. Especially Anne Turnbridge. She'd do these absolute stinkers. And then block the entrance.

So you can imagine how excited we were to get the old gang back together again.

We met in Dean Lipton's shed, which was so dark you could almost imagine we were back in the cubby. And when Anne Turnbridge did this real hummer it was as if nothing had changed at all.

We lit some candles and explained the problem. Good ideas came thick and fast, but none was exactly what we were looking for. Dean suggested we put doggy doos in Bulldog's sandwich, but Robbie said he wouldn't know the difference.

Rick said we should climb onto the school roof and drop a brick on his head, but Anne said that would just make Bulldog madder. Anyway, hurting people is what we were

trying to stop.

And then the perfect idea came. Robbie thought of it. My brother.

Rob was one of those kids who was a really good thinker. He used to think all the time. And sooner or later he would think of something fantastic.

Although I bash Rob up a fair bit, I really love him. Not that I'd ever tell him that, of course.

Rob's idea also involved doggy doos, but not in sandwiches.

'What we have to do,' said Rob, 'is make Bulldog feel like a nerd in front of the whole school. You see, when Bulldog hits you it

hurts, for sure, but I reckon the worst thing is feeling like a nerd because you're too scared to hit back. Humiliated, my dad would say.'

'Let's stick to *nerd*,' said the other kids.

'So,' said Rob, 'if we can make Bulldog feel like we feel, then maybe he won't like it either.'

Makes sense, thought everyone.

'This is what we'll do,' said Rob. 'Each morning, we'll rub just a little bit of doggy doos into Bulldog's bike seat. Sometimes he wears those favourite shorts of his – you know, the daggy ones – three or four days in a row. By the fourth day, things should be looking fairly ugly and that's when we'll get him.'

'How do you mean?' asked the other kids.

'I'll take care of it,' said Rob. 'Wait and see.'

Rob always liked to make us wait and see with his good ideas. It made him excited.

Well, we waited. And waited. For almost a week! But we trusted Rob. And finally the day arrived. It was a hot morning. Really hot. Bulldog arrived wearing his daggy shorts for the fifth day in a row and chucked his bike on the ground. He told Rob to pick it up and put it against the wall for him or he'd punch him out.

'No worries, Bulldog,' said Rob. By the smile on Rob's face I could tell this was the day.

We turned up at morning assembly and then Rob started whispering to the kid in front of him. Soon everyone was whispering. And holding their noses. The sun beat down and the whispering got louder.

'What's going on?' yelled Mr Watson.

'Excuse me, sir,' said Rob, 'but there's a terrible smell and I think I know where it's coming from.'

'And where might that be?' asked Mr Watson.

'From Bulldog, sir,' said Rob.

'How dare you!' shouted Mr Watson.

Kids were busting to laugh but they were too scared of Mr Watson.

'Stand over there facing the wall!' he screamed.

And that should have been the end of it, except Mr Watson started to think that maybe he could smell something too. He sniffed and thought and sniffed again.

Finally it got the better of him and he asked Bulldog to turn around. He looked closely then stepped back in disgust.

'Bulldog, I'm afraid you've had an accident,' said Mr Watson.

Well, you should have heard the laughter. Some kids laughed so much they started rolling on the ground. Even Mr Watson couldn't help a grin.

Poor Bulldog. He checked his shorts, looked around, checked them again, and then just stood there. And went red. And then dark red and then purple.

I don't think I've ever seen anyone look so embarrassed as Bulldog did that hot, smelly, excellent morning.

Well, Rob was right. Bulldog never hurt anyone after that. For a while we had the feeling he wanted to, but he was too scared of what Rob might do next.

These days, Bulldog's not a bad kid. But do you know what? On really hot mornings he checks his bike seat, just in case. I've seen him. But I'd never let him know, of course. And you know what else? I check mine too.

the boy who ran away

Early one morning, Steven Everett checked his watch, quietly slipped into the clothes he'd laid out the night before, grabbed the bag he'd had packed for a week, brushed his teeth, tiptoed into the kitchen and wrote the following note:

Dear Mum, Dad and Anthony,

I'm going. I don't know where but I'm going. When you said the other night that I'm useless, I thought, well, that's it. I've always known how you think Anthony is so good at everything and I'm such a loser and it's so easy to see that you love him and you don't love me.

There must be somewhere I can live where everyone doesn't make me feel like an idiot. Don't worry about me being hungry or anything because I pinched fifty bucks from your purse. Don't worry about Woofer being lost either. I'm taking him with me. At least for now I'll be out of your way. Forever.

Goodbye,

Steven

Steven started to cry but there was no way
he was changing his mind. So he sneaked out
of the kitchen window, crept up to Woofer's
kennel and whispered, 'You ready?'

He let Woofer lick away some tears and took one last look at the house in which he had lived for all of his eleven years. Then he set off down the road.

Steven knew exactly what he would do. Catch a train into the city and just hang around for a while. Until he got himself together. Then he'd find a job, get married and have kids – kids who felt loved.

It didn't take long for Steven to realise that running away wasn't as easy as it sounded.

'No dogs on the train, kid,' said the station master.

'But how am I going to get to the city?' asked Steven.

'Ever heard of walking?' said the jerk station master. 'Either that or you could let the dog play on the tracks for a while. The seven thirty-three's not that far away.'

As the station master turned away, laughing, Woofer peed on his leg.

So, Steven and Woofer did walk. The whole way. Eleven kilometres to the city in the rain.

'Why didn't I bring a coat?' Steven muttered. 'And some food. Everything's so expensive. All I've done is buy a bit of lunch, some dry food for Woof and a few lollies and the money's half gone. Well, a fair few lollies, really, but a bloke gets hungry.'

At last, Steven and Woofer reached the middle of the city. Which was a bit of a worry, really, because once you're standing in the middle, it's hard to think where else to go. It was getting dark, so no good looking for a job until the next day. And it was getting cold, too. Poor old Woofer was a bit scared.

'Don't you worry, Woof,' said Steven. 'You'll be right with me. We'll stick together, OK, Woof?'

Steven would never admit it to Woof, but he was scared too. And cold and wet. Woofer didn't look all that flash either. Time to find somewhere to sleep.

Steven had read in the papers that some

poor street kids have to sleep under bridges. With newspapers for blankets. But he didn't fancy that too much – especially when the kids he saw under one bridge looked pretty tough.

So, Steven and Woofer walked. Anywhere, everywhere, just to keep warm, until finally, Steven's little legs just wouldn't take him any further. He lay down in a park, cuddled into Woofer and fell into a long, shivery sleep.

People saw them still huddled up together the next morning, and of course they called the police. It wasn't very long at all before

Steven was back home again. As quickly as his big adventure had started, it was over.

But it ended just as it had begun. With a note. From his brother Anthony, hidden under his pillow.

This is what it said:

DEAR STEVE,

BECAUSE I'M YOUR BROTHER AND A BOY, I CAN'T SAY MUSHY STUFF TO YOU SO I DECIDED TO WRITE IT DOWN. YOU KNOW HOW MUM AND DAD SAID THEY MISSED YOU REALLY BADLY? WELL, I DON'T KNOW WHETHER YOU BELIEVE THEM OR NOT, BUT THEY DID.

YOU KNOW WHAT ELSE? I MISSED YOU TOO. WORSE

THAN YOU'D EVER BELIEVE. YOU'RE THE BEST BROTHER A KID COULD HAVE.

Do YOU KNOW WHAT'S STUPID? I ALWAYS THOUGHT YOU WERE MUM AND DAD'S FAVOURITE. NOT ME. EVERYONE LIKES YOU, STEVE. EXACTLY AS YOU ARE. BUT ME, I'VE GOT TO TRY ALL THE TIME. I'VE GOT TO MAKE PEOPLE LIKE ME. BY BEING GOOD AT THINGS. YOU KNOW, FOOTY AND SCHOOLWORK AND STUFF.

YOU'RE THE LUCKY ONE. I'D DO ANYTHING TO SWAP. I'VE ALWAYS THOUGHT THAT SECRETLY MUM AND DAD RECKON I'M THE LOSER. THAT'S WHY THEY SAY NICE THINGS WHEN I DO WELL. TO BUILD ME UP.

DON'T EVER RUN AWAY AGAIN, STEVE, I COULDN'T STAND IT. YOU'RE THE ONLY REAL FRIEND I'VE GOT.

ANTHONY

Steven tiptoed to his brother's room and whispered, 'You awake?'

'Yeah,' said Anthony.

'Thanks for the letter,' said Steven.

'That's OK,' Anthony said.

'I am your friend,' said Steven. 'Always. And you know how true friends should be able to say anything to each other?'

'Yeah,' said Anthony.

'If I'm the only real friend you've got,' said Steve, smiling, 'then you're a total loser.'

46

the girl who answered back

'OK,' said Mr Jenkins, 'I want you all to write a story, no more than a page, on what you did during the holidays.'

'What if I don't feel like it?' said Anne Spinks.

'I beg your pardon?' said Mr Jenkins,

more than a little surprised.

'I don't want to do your stupid story,' said Anne.

Mr Jenkins couldn't believe his ears. Anne Spinks was by no means the best-behaved student in class, but she had never been downright rude before.

'What has got into you?' asked Mr Jenkins.

'I should be asking what has got into you,' said Anne. '**A monkey?**'

'Right, that's enough!' yelled Mr Jenkins. 'Stand outside!'

'No,' said Anne.

'**What?**' thundered Mr Jenkins.

'No,' repeated Anne. 'N-O, no!'

Poor Mr Jenkins. He knew he couldn't lay a hand on Anne. He wasn't allowed. Much as he might have wanted to drag her into the corner for time-out, he knew there was no way. And to add to his problem, Anne knew it too.

She'd heard her parents talking about school the night before and how it must be so hard for teachers now that the strap isn't allowed.

'In fact,' said her mum, 'about the only thing poor teachers can do these days is expel kids. Kick them out.'

'So they can be naughty all over again at some other school,' grumbled her dad.

For some reason, Anne Spinks had been feeling bored lately. **Terribly bored.** But hearing her parents' little chat gave her an idea. Suddenly, Anne Spinks didn't feel bored at all.

'All right, Anne,' said Mr Jenkins. 'There are two ways we can handle this. You can explain to me what's going on, or you can sit there until lunchtime and wait for Mrs Noakes to speak to you.'

'Principals don't scare me,' said Anne, rolling her eyes.

'We'll see about that,' said Mr Jenkins, 'because the next step, young lady, is a call to your parents.'

'Don't let me keep you,' said Anne. 'There's a phone in the staff room.'

The other kids didn't know what to think.

'This is awesome,' said Paul Ngu.

'You're an idiot,' said Jessica Wright. 'Mr Jenkins is the best teacher we've ever had and you're just behaving like a jerk.'

'I'm bored,' said Anne.

'Not bored,' said Tessa James. 'Boring.'

The principal did speak to Anne and so did her parents. But it didn't do any good.

'I want a change,' said Anne.

'Is it the schoolwork?' asked her parents. 'Is it too easy?'

'Maybe,' said Anne with a shrug. 'I just

need something different.'

Between you and me, what Anne really needed was a good smack on the bum. Although I shouldn't be saying that anymore, should I? Let's just say that Anne was far too spoilt.

So, the next day, Anne was at it again. She sneaked into the principal's office, grabbed the microphone and said over the loudspeaker:

'Mr Jenkins drinks and smokes,
And does loud burps with
other blokes.'

Next she poured Clag all over Tessa James's lunch, and finally she wrote something very

rude on the blackboard. I can't tell you what it was, but Mr Jenkins wasn't very happy. Not at all.

But there was really nothing he could do. Time went on and Anne became worse. She even went crazy in the school vegetable patch. Chadstone Central Primary School had one of those fantastic programs where kids are allowed to grow fruit and vegetables in the school grounds and then make yummy meals in class. It used to be one of Anne's favourite things to do. But not anymore.

She squashed all the tomatoes in her fingers, kicked the pumpkins (it hurt a bit but she pretended she didn't feel a thing),

snapped all the beans in half, stomped on the strawberries and smashed the blueberries with a garden stake.

'Look,' she said. 'Instant fruit salad.'

Her parents tried their best to calm her down, and Anne knew they were probably right when they said that the best way to beat boredom is to find a new hobby or sport or read a book. But Anne didn't want to find a 'grown-up' answer to her problems. Not just then, anyway. It was as if she'd gone so far down the bad track that to turn back now would make her look foolish.

Finally, Mrs Noakes said, 'Anne, unless your behaviour improves we'll have no choice

but to expel you. You'll have to leave here and go to another school. Do you understand?'

'Understand?' said Anne. 'The sooner the better.'

It was only a short time later that Anne was gone. On her last day, Mrs Noakes tried one last time to talk to her.

'This might seem like a funny thing to say,' said Mrs Noakes, 'but you do realise, I hope, that once you leave here you can never come back?'

'Bonus,' said Anne, crossing her arms.

A year went by and in that time Anne started and quickly finished at three different schools. **All of them boring.** And all the time, although she would never admit to it, those words went around in her head. 'Never come back.'

For some strange reason – maybe because she knew it could never happen – going back to her old school, Chadstone Central, became something she wanted more than anything else in the world.

Over and over again she remembered the time she scored the winning goal against Solway and how they sang all the way home on the bus. The time she cuddled the little kindy kid when she found her crying on her first day. And the time that terribly shy but really nice Richard Hewson asked if he could

walk home with her.

She hadn't seen Richard since she left Chadstone Central. *I wonder what he's doing now?* thought Anne.

Anne even found herself walking home past Chadstone Central, just to have a look at the old place. And she found herself realising that there was nothing wrong with Chadstone Central. Or any other school for that matter. Just something wrong with her.

Late one afternoon, Mrs Noakes was packing her bags to go home when there was a knock at the door.

It was Anne.

'Sorry to bother you,' said Anne, 'but there's something I just have to ask. Please. If that's okay, I mean?'

'Go on,' said Mrs Noakes.

'You know how you said I could never come back,' said Anne. 'Did you really mean it?'

'Yes, I did,' said Mrs Noakes. 'But I can tell the Anne Spinks I spoke to then isn't the same girl I see standing before me now. This one is more than welcome.'

You would never have guessed twelve months ago that Anne Spinks would end up crying and hugging the school principal. And that Mrs Noakes would have a tear in her eye as well.

Bully-Boy 'Boofer' Barnes

When Boofer Barnes started at our school because he'd been kicked out of his old one for bullying, you didn't have to be that smart to see trouble coming our way. Especially when our own school bully, Meat-Head Morgan, said, 'Great. With two of us we

should be able to bash up three times as many kids.'

Good maths, Meat-Head.

To get into our school, Boofer promised that he would change his ways, of course. He'd be a good boy. And they believed him. Der!

Well, it wasn't long before Boofer had every one of us shaking with fear. On the way to school, on the way home, at lunchtime, even in class. From the very first day, Boofer was punching us on the arm, tripping us and spitting on our backs. Giving wedgies, corkies, bockers and headlocks. Jumpers were ripped, rulers snapped, books torn and

school bags thrown over fences.

'Only reason I got kicked out of my old school,' said Boofer, 'is a couple of little sucks dobbed on me. Anyone tries ratting here and they're dead.'

As far as I could work out, Boofer was nasty because he thought the rest of us were a pack of wimps. And wimps deserve to get bashed. Fair enough. We weren't all weakies, of course. It's just that Boofer was twice as big and strong as any kid I'd ever seen. But that didn't seem to have entered his big, fat, ugly head.

Of course, Meat-Head Morgan was most taken with Boofer's thuggery and it wasn't

long before he was thumping everyone even harder than before. And sucking up to Boofer something shocking.

'That kid you just decked,' Meat-Head would ask Boofer. 'Do you want me to jump on him as well? Or knee him or something?'

Like a vulture, he was, hanging around for Boofer's scraps. With Boofer being so huge, even Meat-Head looked small. But for some reason, Boofer let him tag along.

The bullying soon became so bad that some of us found excuses not to go to school. Ear-ache, headache, sick stomach, heart attack…

My father must have cottoned on, because he pulled me aside for a chat. You know how

parents usually don't know anything? Well, sometimes, he did make a bit of sense. He could tell I was scared to go to school and he guessed it was because of bullying.

'There's one thing worth remembering,' he said. 'All bullies are cowards. Gutless. Because they only pick on people smaller than them. People they know they can beat. You watch in a football match. They'll run around whacking everybody from behind but they'll never, ever go into the packs where they might get hurt. They'll never go in for the hard ball.'

Which set me thinking. The very next day at school, having been hit by Boofer again that

morning, I gave everyone the shock of their lives.

'Mrs Cullen,' I asked, 'I think we should have a football match in the next PE lesson. My team against Boofer's team. And I want to play on Boofer because I'm going to show he's got no guts.'

Do you think that didn't cause a stir!

Now, it so happened that I was one of Mrs Cullen's favourite students and although I knew she'd yell at me for being so rude, I also knew that she would probably say yes. And she did. Because she was smart. Although most teachers would have guessed by now that Boofer was up to his old tricks,

no-one had evidence. No-one had actually seen anything or heard any complaints.

So, it was as if Mrs Cullen thought, *I don't know what he's up to, but it's probably worth a try.*

The team I picked was, of course, way better than Boofer's because I was friends with everyone and knew all the best players. My team was so much better, in fact, that we could just about do as we liked. Kick a goal if we felt like it, let them kick one if we didn't. Which was part of my secret plan.

Of course Boofer ran around crunching everyone from behind, just as Dad had said, but he never, ever went into the packs. We

played almost the whole game without doing anything special, just working it deliberately so that the scores were always level.

And then finally the game was almost over. Suddenly, Boofer found himself standing alone with the ball rolling towards him. On my signal, everyone had kept their distance from Boofer, but by now the ball was almost at his feet.

'Get him!' I yelled. 'If he kicks a goal, they win!'

Kids ran from everywhere with fierce looks and bloodcurdling screams. So the pack that Boofer had been avoiding all day was suddenly around him!

We didn't even need to tackle Boofer. Instead of picking the ball up, Boofer turned to jelly. Sooked off completely. He dropped to his knees and covered his head with his arms like a scared rabbit. And then, as the whistle went for the end of the game, Boofer lifted his head to see the rest of us standing in a circle, smiling and laughing, 'Wimp, wimp!'

'I hope you do keep bullying us,' I said to Boofer as we turned to walk away, 'because it will always remind me of the funniest thing I have ever seen in my life. And,' I added, as I took out the camera I just happened to have in my pocket, 'this will make a great photo for the end-of-year school magazine.'

Boofer stayed out on the ground for a very long time, refusing to get changed until we had all left. Everyone, that is, except Meat-Head Morgan. Poor Meat-Head had slipped in the change rooms after the game and torn the nail off his big toe. Life can be so unfair, can't it?

the mystery of Willow Bend

Jane Bransgrove couldn't understand it. 'Why do some people have so much and others hardly have anything? That fat, ugly Lucille Hardy's got a horse, a tennis court, a bike – everything! Yet poor little Emma White has holes in her jumper, holes in

her shoes and holes in her lunchbox where some food should be.'

Emma lived in a caravan park with her mum and four brothers and sisters. She hadn't seen her dad for years. He used to write to her sometimes, but even that stopped. 'He's just really busy,' Emma told Jane.

Jane played with Emma most nights at the caravan park. And there was never anything to eat. Nothing. Girls get hungry after school, but poor Emma's mum never seemed to have any money, even for food. So Emma always looked thin and pale and sad. And Jane was tired of feeling bad about it.

One night, Jane lay in bed thinking. What

could she do to help? Maybe she could sell some of her toys and give the money to Emma's mum. But who'd want a doll's house the dog sleeps in, or old Britney Spears posters?

Perhaps she and Emma could get jobs after school. But where? Jobs were hard enough to get for grown-ups.

Then she thought of it. **Old Billy Dunn.** Billy Dunn was a nice old man who lived next door and used to collect newspapers and bottles and sell them. Until he found something better. Much better. Panning for gold.

'There's plenty of gold still around, if you want to look for it,' Billy was always saying.

'Especially in the hills up the back.'

Jane knew he was telling the truth because Billy had just bought a new truck. So Jane pestered Billy to take her and Emma with him one weekend.

Billy didn't want to, at first. He said it was no place for a little girl. Much too dangerous. There were old mine shafts you couldn't see, snakes, spiders…

'I'm not scared of any of that!' said Jane. 'Emma and I see snakes all the time. At the back of the caravan park.'

'What about your parents?' asked Billy.

'They won't mind,' said Jane. Secretly, she knew they would mind. A lot. So she'd have

to ask them when they were in a good mood.

'Well,' said Billy. 'All right. Just the once. And just to make sure your parents are happy, I'll ask them myself. Tomorrow.'

Jane knew she'd have to work fast. Her best hope, she thought, was to do jobs. Jane hated jobs, but if this was the only way of getting money for Emma, helping out a bit at home wouldn't hurt.

First she tidied her room and then dragged out a pair of undies she'd seen under her bed last week and put them in the wash.

'What's got into you?' asked her mother.

'Oh, nothing,' said Jane. 'You know how I like to help.'

'Do you?' wondered her mother.

'If we all do something,' said Jane, 'it makes it so much easier for everyone.'

Jane's mother didn't know whether to laugh or cry. That's exactly what she'd been saying to Jane for as long as she could remember.

'I think I might clean the toilet now,' said Jane.

Her mother had to hang on to a chair to stop herself from falling over.

Cleaning the toilet was a job Jane hoped she'd never have to do again, ever. She looked in the toilet bowl, almost threw up, and looked at it again. She flushed it. Flushed it again. And then once more.

'There, that should do,' said Jane.

Next, Jane swept the kitchen floor. And that was when her mother said, 'OK, something's going on!'

'No, really, Mum,' said Jane. 'I just thought it was time I grew up a bit.'

Jane could see tears of happiness in her mother's eyes, so she thought she'd better not lay it on **too thick**.

'I really am so lucky to have such a beautiful daughter,' said her mum. 'Give me a big hug.'

And while her mum gave her a cuddle, Jane asked if it would be all right if she and

Emma went gold-panning with Billy on the weekend.

'Yes, of course,' said her mum.

Jane couldn't believe her ears. Her mum had said yes, just like that! How unfair. All those jobs for nothing.

That weekend, Billy, Jane and Emma set out for the hills in Billy's new truck. The girls were excited. It was like a big adventure. Their first chance in life to make mega-bucks!

When Jane explained to Billy that she and Emma wanted to find gold to help Emma's mum, Billy said, 'Well, we'd better go to the

best spot then. My secret spot. Willow Bend. But no telling anyone. Ever. OK?'

'Promise,' said the girls excitedly.

'You never know,' said Billy, as they drove along a bumpy track. 'You girls might bring me luck. You see, there's an old story that says there's still a huge lump of gold out this way that's never been found. The mystery of Willow Bend, I call it. About twenty years ago, this strange old bloke came into the pub and said he'd found a fantastic piece of gold. It was so big he still hadn't found the bottom of it. Of course, he wouldn't tell anyone exactly where it was, but he kept giving us hints. It was as if he wanted to tease us by giving us

little clues. Suddenly he stood on a chair and said this mad poem:

Where the cricket bat turns
Towards the hedge
A tree when it burns
A knife on its edge.'

Billy whistled. 'Why he did that, I don't know. Perhaps he knew he was going to die. Because die he did. The very next day. So as far as I know, the gold's still there. Sure, I find lots of little bits, but never the big one.'

After that story, the girls could hardly wait to start panning and digging! But there was still a little way to drive and after that, a two-kilometre walk.

'What I think,' said Billy, 'is that the poem twists everything around. I've thought about it for years. Take the line where the cricket bat turns. Cricket bats are sometimes made out of willow. And turns could mean bend. Willow Bend.'

'What about towards the hedge?' asked Emma.

'Could be the old hedge up on the hill near Cummings' place,' said Billy. 'The hedge is dead now, but you could definitely see it from Willow Bend. And where the tree burns — well there's plenty of old burnt trees around. But the line I've never been able to work out is a knife on its edge.

I must have thought about it a thousand times.'

Jane and Emma started to think very hard about it, too.

Finally, they arrived at Willow Bend and Billy showed the girls how to pan for gold at the edge of the river. They loved it. The girls didn't find much – in fact none, really – but it was great fun. Especially when Billy fell in. And all the while, around and around in their heads went the line, **a knife on its edge.**

'Edge,' said Emma to herself. 'Edge, sharp, cut, blunt edge...'

'Knife,' said Jane thoughtfully. 'Knife, spoon, fork –'

'Yes!' yelled Billy. 'That's it!'

'What's it?' asked Jane.

'Fork!' said Billy. 'There's a fork in the river just up ahead. And there's a cliff there. That's what he meant. The edge of the cliffs where the river forks.'

Billy wasn't walking up the creek anymore. He was running. Faster then he'd run for years. With the girls at his side.

'Now,' he said puffing, 'here's the fork and there are the cliffs I meant. If I walk up here I can see Cummings' Hedge. It's been twenty years since the poem so the burnt tree will be long gone, but let's start digging anyway!'

Billy was so excited he didn't know

whether to dig or dance or sing or what. But he dug, and so did the girls. Like crazy. Dirt flew everywhere. And sure enough, there soon came a **clink** sound as their spades hit something.

Could this be it? Could this be the piece of gold that would help Emma's mum? The prize that Billy had dreamed about for so many years?

Jane had seen some beautiful things in her life, but she'll never forget the look on old Billy's face when he reached into the ground and pulled out the biggest, shiniest, most fantastic lump of gold you have ever seen. The three of them screamed and laughed and

danced and hugged. And hugged some more.

The people in town couldn't believe it. They were all so excited. 'It couldn't have happened to a nicer bloke,' they said.

'It didn't just happen to me,' said Billy. 'There were three of us. Everything we found is shared.' And they found a lot.

Emma's mum's got some money now. And so has Billy. And Jane too – put in the bank until she's twenty-one. Well, most of it, anyway. Jane went into the city on a small shopping trip. Make that a large shopping trip.

It's important to remember that the three of them discovered something else at Willow Bend that day. A special sort of friendship.

The sort that lasts forever. Which is a lot
longer than money ever lasts.

Write your shopping list on a piece of dunny paper!

ABOUT THE AUTHOR

When successful actor and screenwriter
Christopher Milne became a father, he found
himself reading books at bedtime to his two boys,
Peter and Robert. He soon ran out of stories
to read, so he started making up his own.

He quickly discovered that if he told Pete and Rob
about good boys and girls doing very good things
all the time, they were bored stupid.

But if he told them about naughty kids doing **pooey,**
rotten, disgusting things, his sons would scream for
more. 'We want more of those naughty stories!'

'OK,' Chris would reply. 'But only if you've been good.'
And so the **Naughty Stories for Good Boys and Girls**
were born...

For more info on Christopher Milne and his books, go to
www.ChristopherMilne.com.au